The Teddy Bear
Under the Bed

Aladdin Paperbacks
An imprint of Simon & Schuster Children's Publishing Division
1230 Avenue of the Americas
New York, NY 10020

10 9 8 7 6 5 4 3 2 1

Library of Congress Cataloging-in-Publication Data
Wigand, Molly.
The teddy bear under the bed / by Molly Wigand ; illustrated by Davis Henry.
p.   cm.
Summary: When he goes to scare the bravest girl in town, a young monster is frightened by her teddy bear.
ISBN 0-689-80852-6
[1. Monsters—Fiction. 2. Teddy bears—Fiction. 3. Fear—Fiction.]
I. Henry, Davis, ill. II. Title
PZ7.W6375Te   1996
[E]—dc20
95-53113
CIP   AC

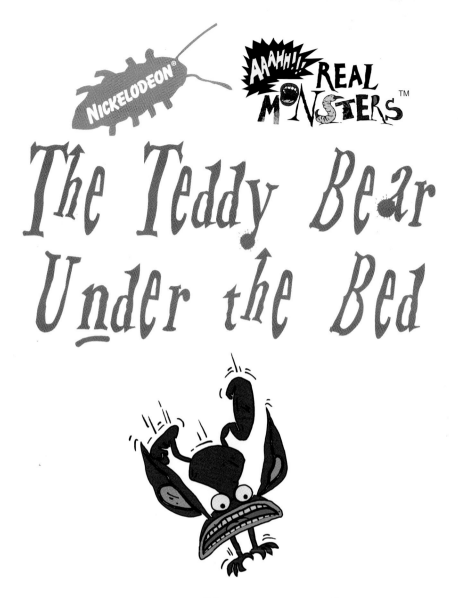

The Teddy Bear Under the Bed

By Molly Wigand

Pictures by Davis Henry

Ready-to-Read
Aladdin Paperbacks

Ickis was excited. He had special homework. His special homework was to find the bravest girl in town and scare her. He tiptoed into town.

Ickis found the bravest girl's house. He
hid in her closet. He waited and waited.
6   At last the girl fell asleep. Ickis jumped out.

"Aaahh!" Ickis yelled.
The girl did not wake up.
"Aaahh!'" he yelled again.
She still did not wake up.

That's when Ickis
saw it. It was big.
It was scary. It was
right there on the
pillow. It was staring
at him.

It was a big, fuzzy,
hairy . . .

. . . cute, cuddly teddy bear!

"Aaahh! Help!" Ickis yelled. He ran for his life.

Ickis ran all the way home.

"Oblina! Krumm!" he said. "You won't believe what I saw!"

"What did you see?" asked Krumm.

"It was terrible. It was horrible. It was cute. It was a teddy bear!"

"Aaahh!" said Krumm.

"Aaahh!" said Ickis.

"Oh, dear!" said Oblina.

13

"Here, Ickis," said Oblina. "Have something to drink. Then you will feel better."

Krumm said, "I hope *I* never see a real teddy bear!"

"Shhh! It is time for bed," said Oblina.
Krumm went to sleep.

Oblina went to sleep.

Ickis closed his eyes. But he could not
sleep. He tried to think of all his favorite
monster things. He tossed and turned.
He turned and tossed.

Then Ickis heard a noise.

A scary something moved under his bed. It sounded big. It sounded hairy. It sounded cute.

"Help!" Ickis screamed. "Wake up!
Wake up!"

"Now what?" asked Oblina.

"A teddy bear is under my bed!"
Ickis cried.

"Are you sure it is a *teddy bear* that
is under your bed?" Oblina asked.

"Y-y-y-yes," Ickis said.

"I do not believe it," Oblina said. "I will see for myself."

"You are one brave monster!"
said Krumm.

Oblina lay on the floor. "Lots of things are hiding under your bed," she said. "Here is a filthy, dirty dust bunny."

"Yum-yum! A bedtime snack!" said
Krumm.
He grabbed the filthy, dirty dust bunny.

Oblina reached under the bed again.

"Look!" she said. "A sticky, icky cobweb."

"Dessert!" said Krumm. He grabbed the
sticky, icky cobweb. Then he closed his eyes.

"I see just one more thing under here," Oblina said.

"I knew it," said Ickis. "It's a cute teddy bear."

"No," said Oblina. "It is not a teddy bear.
It is a big, fat, slimy, grimy worm."
 Ickis hugged the worm. "Thanks,
Oblina," he said. "Now I feel safe."

"Good night," said Ickis.

"Good night, Ickis and Krumm," said Oblina. "Sleep tight."

Then Oblina said softly, "Good night,
teddy monster." And all the monsters
went to sleep.

If you liked this book, look for these other books featuring the *Real Monsters!*

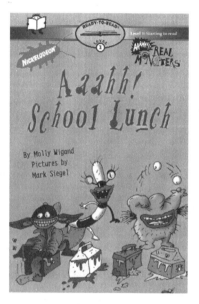

Aaahh! School Lunch
by Molly Wigand
illustrated by Mark Siegel
ISBN 0-689-80853-4
A Ready-to-Read book: Level One

The Curse of Katana
by H.P. Gilmour
ISBN 0-689-80870-4

The Switching Hour
by Joanne Barkan
ISBN 0-689-80851-8